FOR GELA, MICHAEL AND MAX
SMALL HUGS FOR MONIKA AND LUKA

HODDER CHILDREN'S BOOKS

First published in Great Britain in 2019
by Hodder and Stoughton

Text and illustrations copyright © David Melling, 2019

The right of David Melling to be identified
as the author and illustrator of this Work has been
asserted by him in accordance with the Copyright,
Designs and Patents Act 1988.

A CIP catalogue record for this book
is available from the British Library.

HB ISBN: 978 1 444 92510 4
PB ISBN: 978 1 444 92511 1

1 3 5 7 9 10 8 6 4 2

Printed and bound in China

MIX
Paper from
responsible sources
FSC® C104740
FSC
www.fsc.org

Hodder Children's Books
An imprint of Hachette Children's Group
Part of Hodder and Stoughton
Carmelite House
50 Victoria Embankment
London, EC4Y 0DZ

An Hachette UK Company

www.hachette.co.uk
www.hachettechildrens.co.uk

www.davidmelling.co.uk

www.huglessdouglas.co.uk

HuGLESS DouGLAS
and the
BABY BIRDS

David Melling

h
Hodder
Children's
Books

Douglas was counting his spring collection.

So far he had

two leaves,

one smooth stone,

a funny-shaped twig . . .

and a busy caterpillar

that wouldn't keep still.

Suddenly there was a crashing noise and a nest landed on his lap followed by a squirrel.

'I didn't know squirrels laid eggs!' said Douglas.

'We don't!' said Squirrel. 'It's Swoopy Bird's nest and it bumped right into me!' Before Douglas could reply, Squirrel had disappeared.

'Oh my,' called Swoopy Bird.
'My nest, my eggs, my babies!
What am I going to do?'

'Don't worry,' said Douglas,
'your eggs are safe but I think
you might need a new nest.'

Swoopy Bird asked Douglas to look
after her eggs while she quickly
built a new nest.

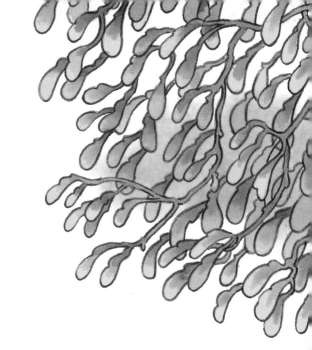

Douglas agreed. He watched for
a while, then sat down. 'I'll wait
right here,' he said.

The trouble with waiting, thought Douglas,

is the **sitting** **still** part.

It gives me the fidgets.

Just then he thought he heard whispering . . .

It was the Funny Bunnies!
'Hello,' said Douglas. 'I'm looking after
Swoopy Bird's eggs while she builds a
new nest. Do you want to help?'

'My mum says birds' eggs must be warm, that's why they sit on them,' said a little bunny.

'Maybe I should sit on these,' said Douglas.

'NOOOO!'

cried the Funny Bunnies.

Another bunny put his arms around a bit of Douglas. 'I feel safe and warm when someone hugs me.'

'EGG HUGS!'

cried the Funny Bunnies.

'OK, but you'll have to be very gentle.' said Douglas.

So   every   bunny   was

given   one   egg each   to hug.

After a while, they put the warm
eggs back in the old nest.

'I think they're ready to hatch!'
said Douglas excitedly.

'What does that mean?' asked the bunnies.
'It's when the baby birds come out of
their eggs,' he said.

And sure enough, they did.
Soon, there were EIGHT
FLUFFY
BIRDS

with very quick runaway legs.

'Oh no!' cried Douglas.
'Can anyone see them?'

A family of sheep were passing
by and stopped to help.

Suddenly Squirrel appeared.
'Douglas, do you know you have
a bird on your head?' he asked.

From up in the tree, Squirrel could spot all eight
babies and pointed them out to everyone.

LUCKILY, it didn't take long to gather them and put them back in the old nest.

'Phew!' said Douglas. 'Thank you, Squirrel.'

High above, Swoopy Bird
was **so excited** to see her
baby birds had hatched.
'Just in time,' she chirped.
'The new nest is ready!'

Douglas and his friends made themselves into a wobbly ladder, and even Squirrel joined in.

And after a bit of **up**
and a bit of down . . .
the birds were safely
in their new home.

'My babies are back,'
cried Swoopy Bird,
and gave them a
FAMILY HUG.

She was so happy she hopped from
branch to branch to give everyone a
THANK-YOU HUG.

After all the excitement, Douglas sat down to play with his spring collection. He now had some feathers and a few egg shells.

But his friends had another idea . . .

'Let's have a
DAISY-CHAIN HUG!'
they cried.

'Perfect for a spring day!' laughed Douglas.

THINGS TO SPOT ON A SPRING DAY:

Baby birds that have left the nest

Baby birds

Fluffy cloud shapes

Baby lambs

Bird spotters

Colourful flowers

Busy bees

Bird song

Caterpillars and butterflies

A squirrel's nest

Tree blossom

New seedlings

Nesting birds

Crawly insects

April showers

MAKE YOUR OWN SPRING FRIENDS!

YOU WILL NEED:

Cut-out paper eyes

Feathers

Leaves

Sticks and twigs

Stones

Along with pencil, paper, scissors
and an adult to help.

1. Take a bag when you go for a nature walk
and collect twigs, leaves, small stones, feathers and
anything else you find interesting.

Tip: Try and collect lots of different shapes and sizes.

2. Cut out two or three pairs of eyes from paper
and draw dots in the middle.

3. Mix and match! Arrange the different pieces
together and try and create your spring friends or
make up new ones!

Note: Only use things that you see lying on the floor.
Don't pick anything that is growing!

HERE ARE SOME FRIENDS TO GET YOU STARTED!